MORE HALLOWEEN HOWLS

RIDDLES THAT COME BACK TO HAUNT YOU

by Giulio Maestro

DUTTON CHILDREN'S BOOKS

NEW YORK

8818
Maestro

Copyright © 1992 by Giulio Maestro

Library of Congress Cataloging-in-Publication Data

Maestro, Giulio.
More halloween howls: riddles that come back to haunt you/by Giulio Maestro.
p.   cm.
Summary: A collection of riddles about witches, vampires, skeletons, and other scary Halloween creatures.
ISBN 0-525-44899-3
1. Riddles, Juvenile.   2. Halloween—Juvenile humor.   3. Wit and humor, Juvenile
[1. Halloween—Wit and humor.   2. Riddles.]
I. Title.
PN6371.5.M274   1992
818.5402—dc20   91-23505   CIP   AC

Published in the United States by Dutton Children's Books,
a division of Penguin Books USA Inc.
375 Hudson Street, New York, New York 10014

Printed in Hong Kong by Wing King Tong Co., Ltd.
First Edition   10 9 8 7 6 5 4 3 2 1

HALLOWEEN HOWLS

Why are black cats such good singers?
They're very mewsical.

What's a cold, evil candle?
The wicked wick of the north.

What do you call a little fruit who plays tricks?

Berry bad.

Why was the skunk's car smelly to drive?

It had an automatic stink shift.

What kind of hot dogs do werewolves like best?

Hallowieners.

How does a cow read at night?
By moolight.

Where do little ghosts learn to yell "BOO!"?

In noisery school.

How do you get stuck in muck?
Jog in a bog.

Why does a skeleton always use an umbrella?
It likes to stay bone-dry.

What do fangs do to french fries?
Turn them into gnashed potatoes.

What does a goblin shop for?
Grosseries.

How can you tell when windows are scared?

They get shudders.

What do you call serious rocks?
Grave stones.

Why did the witch stand up in front of the audience?

She had to give a screech.

What does a healthy sorcerer eat?
Supernatural foods.

What's a goblin's favorite flavor?
Lemon 'n' Slime.

Why wasn't the vampire working?
He was on his coffin break.

How do ghosts fly from one place to another?

By scareplane.

How do you picture yourself flying on a broom?

By witchful thinking.

What's a ghoul's favorite breakfast cereal?

Rice Creepies.

What's a ghastly dessert?
Dread pudding.

Why did the witch's mail rattle?
It was a chain letter.

Why did the vampire's lunch give her heartburn?

It was a stake sandwich.

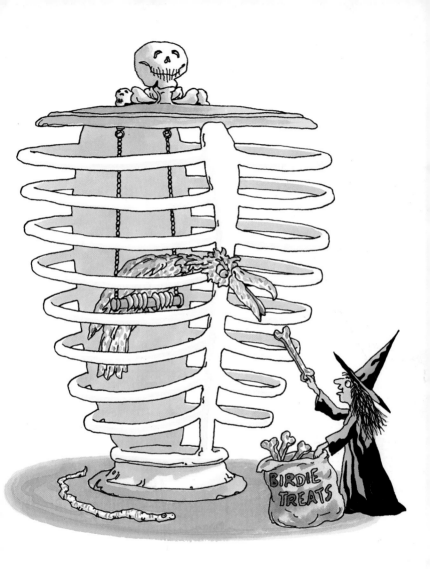

What do you call a bony birdhouse?
A rib cage.

What instrument does a skeleton play?
The trombone.

Why was the zombie so grumpy?
She woke up too early in the mourning.

What directions did the ghost give the goblin?

"Make a fright turn at the corner."

Why was the witch fond of
her snake?

He had a pleasant poisonality.

What's a black cat's favorite dessert?
Mice pudding.

What do birds give out on Halloween?
Tweets.

What did the witch get at
the beauty parlor?

A hair-raising experience.

What's a vampire's favorite feast?
Fangsgiving Day dinner.

What do little trees say on Halloween?

"Twig or treat."

When does a night sky sound scary?
When there's a full moan.

How does a skeleton feel in the snow?

Chilled to the bone.

What's an extra-large Halloween dessert?

Plumpkin pie.

Why did the snake clean the car's front window?

It was a windshield viper.

Why was the skeleton a good student?

It had an open mind.

What kind of soda does a frog like?
Croaker Cola.

What's creepy about chilled shellfish?
They're cold and clammy.

What does a vampire suck on for a sore throat?

Coffin drops.

When is a wizard like a UFO?
When he's a flying sorcerer.

Why did the dragon wake up frightened?

He had an alarming clock.

Why was the werewolf afraid of the girl?

She was Little Red Rotten Hood.

What do goblins mail home while on vacation?

Ghostcards.

Why did the vampire need
mouthwash?

She had bat breath.

Why did the monster stay on a diet?
To keep her ghoulish figure.

Where do toads hang up their coats?
In the croakroom.

What does a vampire call
a tasty treat?

"Fangtastic!"

What did the coldhearted monster
have for lunch?

Peanut brrrrr and jelly.

Where does a spider check her spelling?

In Cobwebster's Dictionary.

What does a cool ghoul eat?
Chilly dogs.

Why did the music make the
monster sick?

It had a catchy malady.

What do you call admiring letters to a vampire?

Fang mail.

What's a Halloween lunch?

A sandwitch.

Why was a hat in the graveyard?
It was on a headstone.

How can you tell how much
a lizard weighs?

Check the scales.

What holiday is a hoot?
Owloween.

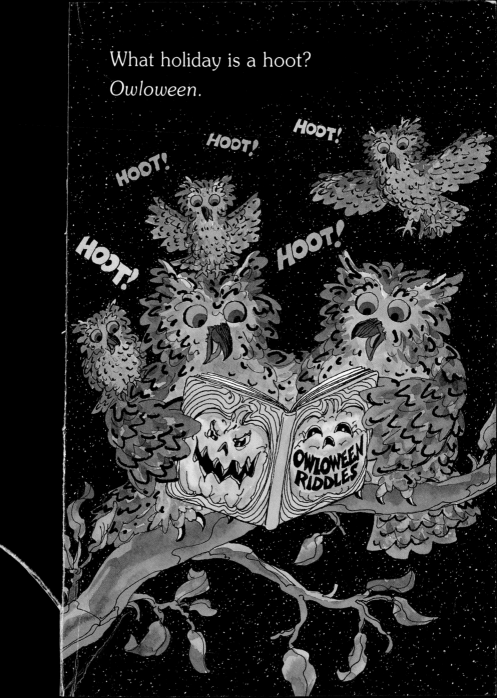